What If?

By: Melanie Hendricks-Richert

2011

ISBN # 9781466438651

A Special Thank You!

I have to thank my wonderful husband Fred and my two lovely children, Freddie and Cecelia. Life is so much happier with the three of you in it.

Also, this book would not have been possible if it wasn't for those that provided me with the experience. Thank You!

I am also very blessed, because of my family and friends. I hope this book inspires all of you to live without regrets and to take a risk.

I dedicate this book to my mother Cindy, for her guidance before and after her death. Even though she is not here with me physically, she is definitely here with me in my heart!

What If?

Chapter 1

I know that everyone has experienced it. That feeling that doesn't go away every time someone brings it up or your memory gets triggered by something that pertains to it. It is a horrible wonder that you will never know the ending to, because your heart or fate didn't allow you to take the risk. How would life have turned out? Would you be better or worse off? It is something you will never have the answer to. This is where my story begins...

What would you expect from the way that I grew up? It wasn't all about being prim and proper, sipping tea, and acting lady-like. It was all about trying to keep up in a man's world. I credit my upbringing on making me a strong woman and allowing me to go out on paths that were right for me. I wasn't going to live my life waiting on someone else, but I was going to set out on my own and figure out what life had to offer. It was difficult trying to fit in and find my place in the world amongst those that had everything handed to them and others that tried everything to stay afloat.

I was caught in between these two worlds just trying to get by. My life was not perfect and that I have never claimed to be true, however all of my life's experiences have taught me to be my own person, not to expect others to do it for me, and to allow my decisions to take me to the place that I am now. With all of these experiences, I also allowed myself to love. Love is a powerful thing. It can make or break you in a way that can be utterly devastating or allow you to keep pushing on to find it again.

This all began in a small rural town in Northwestern North Dakota. On the main drag there was enough God and beer to keep your life in order, depending which way you turned to get your problems solved. The people were simple, kind, and loved to keep a watchful eye on everyone's kids. The saying "it takes a village to raise a child," this was very true. Some knew when to turn their heads and let teens be teens, while others enjoyed nailing the cop's kid to the signs that had holes in them out on Highway 40, or the time when the old church North of town got broken into, or when Mr. Whipple's cows got let out of the pasture, and also when Claire and I wrote in red lipstick the word "slut" on that good for nothing's car.

If you told one person what you did on the weekend, you would be sure to know that that one person told ten others who told their dad who happens to sit at the same table as your dad enjoying morning coffee at the local café. It never failed. Then I would have to come up with a good explanation why someone would have the audacity to think that it could have been me?

Small towns have their good qualities, but when you are an invincible teenager a small town doesn't always work out in your favor.

My family consisted of my dad, my brother, and myself. We were not your typical family, we were borderline dysfunctional. The only thing that was not dysfunctional was how much we all loved one another. Our dad was the local lawman that was highly respected for being fair and just. He was well known to have a large collection of guns that were loaded anytime the opposite sex would show up at the house looking for me. Let's just say I didn't have guys knocking down the door asking me out!

My brother Jeff is older than me. He taught me everything I needed to know about how to get away with anything and everything. He was rough around the edges, but kind when he had to be. He did quite well keeping the boys away from his little sister.

Last but not least, there was me. I was a plain Jane. I was not drop-dead gorgeous, popular, or a queen of anything except my castle. I was mostly a tomboy. I would rarely put on a dress for a special function if it was warranted. This wasn't the way it always was.

Our mother was tragically killed in a motor vehicle accident when a semi crossed the center line. It was the worst thing that could happen to all of us. She was the cream of the crop. She loved our dad and she lived for us kids. It was devastating to say the least. The whole town felt our pain. We were given a lot of support from the local churches as well as our friends. This was the one thing that made our town special. There was always someone that was bringing over food and giving us something that we needed.

Many people wondered what would ever become of Jeff and me, but we knew that we would be just fine if we all stuck together. It was going to be tough, but we would learn to carry on.

Being a teenage girl without a mom was not ideal. There were things that have yet to happen to me and I had no one to talk too.

Girls were mean and dad did not have the time to deal with who wanted to be my friend this week and who decided they didn't the next. His way of parenting was tough love, military style. Don't cry, don't place pity on yourself, suck it up, and move on. Jeff was not one to have girl talk with me either. He was too busy juggling his many girlfriends to care about what was going on with me. Dad even tried to send me away to live with one of my aunts, because it would be easier for me to grow up with a motherly figure. I refused to leave. My place was with the two of them. After all we were grieving together. I also felt like it was my job to watch over them. I was the woman of the house now and I had to make sure that they were cared for.

At night I would pray that life would get easier, that I could leave this town and not become a lifetime waitress at the local café. Not that this was a horrible career choice, it just wasn't for me.

I had hopes and dreams for myself, for my life. I prayed that I would be rescued from this hell. I don't think that I actually prayed to God, but prayed that my mother would hear me. "Please mom, come to me and give me advice. I don't know what to do." I was so angry at God. How dare he take away my mother! Didn't he know that I needed her to be there for me? I hadn't even fallen in love yet. A girl needs her mother for a number of reasons. A mother needs to tell her daughter to hold on to her heart and to not give it to some worthless high school boy, but to save it for someone that she is truly in love with. One that won't take her for granted, but see how special she is. Let's be honest, there is not one high school boy that would think that a girl that gives it up to him, is giving him something sacred. It is just another notch on his belt.

A mother provides a soft comfort to her children, a safe place to cry, to share their worries, and to allow them to grow and spread their wings. A mother is a child's best cheerleader. I was missing this.

My mother was a lovely woman with a big heart. She taught me how to make cookies, do my hair, be a girly girl, and was there for me when I started developing. Thank God, because I can't imagine what it would have been like if it was just dad. He probably would have made me march over to his friend's house to speak with his wife about what changes were taking place with my body.   How embarrassing! It was bad enough that Jeff was around for everything to happen. Acne, braces, and the ugly stage all took place with my mom still there to provide support. I guess this happened at the right time, because soon after all of these stages either started or ended she was gone.

I always thought that when it came to boys I would have the upper hand. I was the ultimate catch. I could load a gun, shoot deer, fish, and I didn't mind getting dirty. This was my new way of life. If I wanted to experience anything, I had to do what my dad and Jeff were doing.

Hunting season would come and I could see the pride in dad's eyes. After all, he taught me everything I knew. Even though I didn't shoot a deer, I provided dad with great stories to share with his friends like how I forgot to take the safety off, and how I got gun shy when a 9 point buck was standing broadside right in front of me. Jeff always added to the excitement of the stories too, like how he would stand right behind me and whisper in my ear "shoot it" or "what are you waiting for?" Dad would tell his friends about all of my near misses and how maybe next year Savannah will tag the big one.

Jeff was a great shot and of course he nailed a deer the first day of the opener. Even though I had to hear the great story about how Jeff snuck up on his deer and pegged it before it knew he was there, it was well worth it. This meant that Jeff's super cute friends would be coming over to help him butcher his deer.

I would sit out in the garage and watch them carefully dismantle the deer carcass, only to take a break to spit their dips into a bottle. To most girls of class, this would be disgusting, but I knew it was part of being a man. Jeff's friend Kyle always asked me if I would like to take part in chewing

Copenhagen with the boys. I always replied with a firm "no!" I enjoyed the smell of it coming off of their breaths not from mine. I saw myself as one of the boys, but that would have gone too far.

This one time, Kyle thought it would be funny to run me down with Copenhagen in one hand, sit on me, and shove a big ol' dip right in the bottom of my lower lip. Despite dry heaving, it was kind of nice having Kyle touch me. He was very good looking. He was all Cowboy from head to toe. He wore tight Wrangler jeans, cowboy boots, and even had a mark from his Copenhagen can in his back pocket. He drove a big loud truck, and was hot. Because of him, I bought my first pair of cowgirl boots and my first pair of bareback Wrangler jeans. I was trying to appeal to his western sense of style.

Kyle was my first crush or should I say my first infatuation. It wasn't love or anything like that, but I was physically attracted to him. Every girl getting ready to graduate high school needs to have at least one object of infatuation. Isn't that a rite of passage?

Another thing I enjoyed more than Kyle was spending time with my friends. After all, they were the ones that kept me sane. We would spend long hours talking about our interests, usually boys, and what our plans would be after graduation.

Most of them were planning on attending local community colleges and staying close to home. They had family in the area and didn't feel the need to bolt like I did. I dreamed of a life far from here. I needed more opportunity and a chance to find myself. Even though leaving this area meant leaving my first crush Kyle, I knew there were bigger plans for me. Kyle was never going to leave this one horse town. He had obligations that tied him to this area forever. And besides, we were not even close to being attached. Hell, we weren't even a couple. If anything Kyle would provide an out for me. There was no way I was going to graduate still a virgin. It would be no strings attached. You take it away from me and then we go our separate ways.

My friends thought I was crazy. Why spend so much time making this plan with Kyle when there was someone else that was more worthy. This other guy was actually interested in me. We did have that time in the culvert. We swapped a little spit and it was really good. Not too bad when you teach yourself how to French kiss on the back of your hand thanks to the instructions from a Cosmo magazine!

Of course this was a secret, and a hard one to keep. I don't know what it was about him, but he made my heart skip a beat. Grant always had a special place in my heart. I never knew if he felt anything or if I was just a good person to practice with. After all, practice made perfect! Grant wasn't a jock, cowboy, or some Greek god. He was just Grant. He was kind, cute, funny, flirty, and good at a lot of things, a jack-of-all-trades. He was smart and had a great future ahead of him. On lucky occasions we would find ourselves together.

This whole situation made me yearn for some motherly advice. I had no one. The one time that I tried talking to a family friend, she went and told my dad everything. I was even hypothetically speaking and she still told him that I just might be crushing on some boy and it might be time to have "the talk" with me. I was so embarrassed and hurt. How dare she do that to me! Dad was the type to make sure there was absolutely no dating, no boys calling, and I was never to buy any article of clothing that would enhance any part of my figure.

Who would I talk to? Of course, I had girlfriends, but they were allowed to do everything that I wasn't. They had mothers. They would be so kind to share the advice that their mothers gave them. "Savannah, just don't get pregnant!" Well I hadn't even thought that far ahead. You can't get pregnant if you don't have anyone that wants to have sex with you. But boy did I feel the pressure. Everyone was having sex, even Jeff!

I remember on prom night, Dad and Jeff were in the office. Dad passed Jeff a condom and said "son, tonight is a big night, you know what this is, so use it and be safe." Jeff had a 2 a.m. curfew and mine was 11 p.m. This was not fair by any means. If I was going to experience anything, I would have to be good enough to get it completed in a short amount of time.

My chance came one night when we were out at a wedding dance. Wedding dances were sometimes the only entertainment that this town offered. There were tons of people out getting drunk and having a great time. Jeff and Kyle came home from college and I thought why not this is the perfect setting. Lots of distractions, no one will notice if Kyle and I sneak out and that is when I will seal the deal.

Grant was there too. He was dating someone that I secretly despised. She was all wrong for him. What did he see in her? From what I could see, she was only good for one thing! Didn't Grant and I have a connection? It's not every day that you make out with a chic in a culvert. That was special. I hope she knows that he is a great kisser, because I taught him everything he knows! Not to mention, when they are together he searches the crowd for me!

Enough about Grant, tonight was the night that the pressure I was experiencing was going to ease off and I would leave for college less "intact." I hadn't even seen a penis in real-life other than in my Health class textbook. Not even my best guy friend would show me his! He wouldn't even help a girl out! I was about to step into unchartered territory with no prior inspection.

The wedding dance was a great place to break the ice and to get Jeff to back off of his comrade. Tonight it was about me and Kyle getting down and dirty. No strings attached and smooth sailing from here on out. I danced with Kyle to every slow song possible to make Grant jealous. Then we ditched the party to head out back. I was physically attracted to Kyle, so of course this would help my cause. He was cute, tall, and ready to get this show on the road.

I wondered if Kyle even knew I had a vagina. I mean, I was always doing guy things and not exactly dressed in the latest fashions. Well I guess, he was going find out. Tonight I was a young girl, ready to become a young woman, self taught and ready to see what was lurking underneath the zipper of Kyle's Wranglers. He was full of testosterone and of course he could be the hero. He could take away my virginity. It was a win-win for the both of us. I was dressed to the nines in a short skirt with my cowgirl boots, and a shirt that I changed into out in my vehicle, so it wouldn't get disapproval from dear old dad. I was feeling like Sandy from the movie "Grease." I was feeling beautiful, sexy, and ready to get it on.

Kyle sensed that I was ready to partake in a little forbidden play on the back of his tailgate and then move the party into a less conspicuous spot.

Kyle put his arm around my waist and ushered me to his truck. We began to kiss and hands were moving all over the place. It was great. He was a little sloppier at kissing then Grant, but who was keeping score. Kyle moved his hand to his zipper and undid it. He then placed my hand straight down the inside of his boxers to play with what was lurking on the inside. Oh my God...What do I do now? Kyle grabbed my hand to make sure it wouldn't sneak out. There it was a full blown hard-on. Oh...I read about this in Cosmo. "How to give your man a hand-job that will blow his mind." I tried to ignore it, but he kept making sure my hand was grasping it with full force. The skin was so soft. I think Kyle's first lover was his left hand and a bottle of lotion.

His kisses were softer now and his lips parted to moan with delight. I thought in my head "I've got you by the balls now." I owned him. I had his most sensitive asset in my hand right this very minute. He wanted me and I wanted him. It was the perfect combination for losing something I had carried around for 18 years. This obviously wasn't his first time. He instructed me on what to do and then asked me to "suck it." Whoa! This was way out of my scope of practice. This had to be next month's issue. I was not ready for this. I guess if this is what he wanted it was only fair to oblige. I wanted him to do something for me, so I guess it was even. Just as I was getting ready to wrap my lips around it, Jeff walked up with his weekend girlfriend. Busted! Nothing like having your brother catch you in the act.

This was unfortunately not going to be the night that I lost my virginity. After Jeff busted us, Kyle shriveled up like a turtle head going back into its shell. There was no way we were going to rekindle the fire that was flaring prior to getting busted. Kyle and I shared a special moment. One that we vowed we would start back up the next time he came back to town.

Kyle got a bad case of blue balls and I got my first glimpse of the male genitalia up close and personal. I was impressed that Kyle was able to shove it back into his tight jeans. It was actually quite impressive or maybe because I had nothing else to compare it to. Either way, it was a great learning opportunity.

Chapter 2

As the school year progressed, it was time to start making other more important decisions. Life couldn't revolve around Kyle, Grant, and my new knowledge. I needed to think about college. Where would I go? What would I study? I was interested in Veterinary Science. If I chose this, it would mean moving to a larger city to attend a University. This is where I belonged now. I wanted to get away from here and this was my ticket out.

I found myself praying to my mother for guidance. Dad was not much help. He felt that the best decision was to attend a local college, to save money for life after school, and to not rack up so much debt. I think he just wanted to keep an eye on me. He would warn "Savannah, big cities are dangerous and full of crime." I wanted to get away from his clutches and try to find myself. I was not born to stay in a small town and live a mediocre life. I was driven, I was determined, and I was going to make something of myself. I had a lot to prove, not just to everyone else, but to myself. I had what it took to be successful.

Kyle came back a few more times before graduation. He didn't get what he wanted from me, so he moved on. I was still very much a virgin. I heard a story that Kyle and some virgin chic screwed and she bled like a stuffed pig. He was completely grossed out and never let anyone let it go. I guess that by Jeff walking in on us, it saved me a lot of heartache. Who knows what would have happened to me the first time? Thank God, my first time wasn't going to be with him. I needed someone that was going to be kind and tender. There was nothing tender about Kyle. It wasn't making love for him, it was pure fucking.

Graduation night was here. I longed to hear how proud my mom was of me, and how happy she was that I stayed true to myself. It was time for me to spread my wings and fly. Instead, I had Dad telling me to rethink my decisions and that North Dakota had great schools and I didn't have to go so far away. This made me want to run. Get as far away as possible. He obviously didn't see my potential or let alone see I wanted something more for myself. There was definitely a lack of support. Did he really think that I would be okay living here? When in my whole life, I talked about living in a big city and wanting the fast paced lifestyle.

After my graduation party that was a success, thanks to my aunts, I headed out on the town. I was ready to spend the last night of my high school days with the people that I had known forever. I got all dressed up and ready for a great time.

I spent most of the night laughing and reminiscing with friends. It didn't matter what was being talked about, someone just had to bring up the fact that I had been missing out on having my mother there with me. Claire said "Savannah, your mom is shining down on you right now, she would have been so proud." Just like that my eyes filled with tears. I really could have used her around these last couple of months. I hopped off the tailgate to find a quiet, safe place to cry. This was far from easy.

God I missed her. I don't even know what life would have been like if she hadn't died that night. I have done everything, dishes, ironing, washing clothes for everyone, making sure Dad and Jeff didn't throw punches, learning to be more like Dad's second son, hunting, and fishing. I had to teach myself how to put on make-up, do my hair, and dress like a girl. I had to seek out advice on friendships, boys, and other things from the articles in YM and Cosmo magazines. This was not normal. This was not how my friends had it. They had the latest and the greatest fashions, shoes, a shoulder to cry on, and never ending amounts of motherly advice. They didn't have to work full-time during the "best days of their lives." I was utterly heartbroken. Mom has missed this huge milestone in my life and there would be more to come.

Just as the tears began streaming down my cheeks, Grant walked up to me. I hurriedly wiped the tears that had streamed down my powdered cheeks. It was no use, he knew I was crying. The redness in my eyes gave it away. Grant put his arms around me. This felt so comforting. It was just what I needed in a time like this. It was as though his arms were meant to hold me. We just fit. He kissed my forehead and wiped my cheeks with his flannel shirt. It smelled so good.

"I know this is really hard on you." "I am so proud of you getting into school. "You will be a great vet." "I will miss you so much, your laugh, and your smile." "I guess this may seem weird, but we always seem to find each other." I agreed with him. Once my eyes came back into focus, I looked around to see if his girlfriend was watching what was going on. She was nowhere to be found. Luckily for me, I was going to sit back and let whatever was about to happen, happen. My heart was pounding. I wondered if he could feel it pressed up to his chest. I guess this was my body's way of saying "look what he does to you!" I wanted him, right then and there. It was always Grant. I never should have been wasting my time with Kyle. At this affirmation, I kissed him as passionately as I could. And he kissed back. I swear there were fireworks going off. This felt perfect. Not only did his arms fit with my body, his lips and mine were like two puzzle pieces joining together. This was a special moment. Just when we broke off the kiss and were still locked together in an embrace, his ugly girlfriend showed up. Once again, I was busted. She walked up to us and glared at me. She had seen everything. He was busted and so was I. Why not? I deserved to be caught red-handed. He was spoken for. He wasn't mine. I had no right treading on her turf. Once again, I was left heartbroken, but this time it was different. There were legit feelings between both of us. I knew he felt it. The intensity was out of this world. He looked into my eyes, but not only that, he touched my soul. He had my heart in his hands. "I love you Grant!" These words would have to wait. This was by far not the time to confess my true feelings for him and get my ass kicked all at the same time by his not so cute girlfriend. He just walked away from me like a scolded puppy. Would we ever get this chance again? I guess only time would tell.

Claire saw everything. She could tell this was not going to help my mood. My life was like a rollercoaster. Happy-Sad-Happy-Sad. When would it be my turn? I needed to catch a break. I was starting to think that I would always be alone. I don't think Grant was in love with her. I think he felt sorry for her and she went out of her way to please him. After all, he was the only one that would pay any attention to her. I wished she would fall off the face of the Earth! I really shouldn't think that, but that is how I felt. Hopefully, she wasn't blind and could see he kissed me back too! If he didn't feel anything for me, he would have humored me with a lifeless kiss. There was nothing lifeless about it.

Oh well, this was not the night that I would get to see if Grant and I were going to be wrapped up in an embrace until the morning sun woke us up. Instead, he was probably going to go home with her and give her sympathy sex to smooth everything over. This just made me sick to my stomach. I just blamed it on the blackberry brandy and 7-Up concoction. Truly, it was the thought of him getting it on with that ugly bitch. Oh I just hated her. The sad part of it, she wasn't ugly. She was cute and I was jealous. She had something that I wanted and it killed me to see them together. This whole situation was a stupid waste of time, but shame on him for kissing me.

Claire said that I needed to clear my head of all of this nonsense and enjoy my last night with everyone. It was so hard to put all of this on the backburner. But I had too. I needed to stay focused on what was really important to me and that was finishing the summer with no more heartbreak and getting the hell out of town.

Chapter 3

Summer was ending and my new life was just around the corner. Good thing, because I was sick of working at the gas station and dealing with stupid people.

Grant ignored me, but when our eyes would meet in passing I knew he had regrets. He wanted to finish what we started and so did I.

"Well my car is all packed, fueled, and ready to hit the road." "I am ready to blow this popsicle stand!" Dad had tears in his eyes, but he stayed strong. Heaven forbid, he sends me off with a "I'm proud of you Savannah, you will do great." "Just remember, you always have a place to come home too." Instead he gives me a hug, a phone card, and a couple hundred dollar bills in case of an emergency.

As I pull out, I give him a final wave as tears pour down my cheeks. The tears cloud my vision, but I have pulled out of this driveway so many times, it doesn't matter if I can see clearly or not. I give myself a pep talk. "Cheer up Savannah!" "This is a moment you have been waiting for." I am probably the only Freshmen virgin and besides Grant had his chance to tell ugly goodbye and hello Savannah. He just chose not to. Life would go on. It was time for me to hit the big city with my dreams in full view, my options wide open, and my wings ready to fly.

This time I prayed to God for safe travels and thanked my mom for guiding me down this path. Whoever said that I didn't believe in God is full of shit. God does answer prayers. I have a car full of fuel ready to take me out of this town. I have my whole life ahead of me to experience things that I could never do in this town under the watchful eye of the local vigilantes. And not to mention, I am ready to allow God to show me my full potential. What this life has to offer! I am going to be helping God's creatures in my line of work. That should prove something, right? In my mind, I didn't need to be a bible banger to do God's work. I was doing something that I loved with my life. That should amount for something. Not only that, it looked like I would be saving myself for marriage. That was just one more thing that proved that I was a good Christian girl. I will be honest, God and I have our issues, but I am learning that things don't just fall into place. They get put there in front of you, because a higher power wants you to succeed.

I got into the city after dark. The lights are spread as far as my eyes can see. It was a little overwhelming, but I felt like I could do this. I would find my way around and take in what the city had to offer. This was it, sink or swim.

School starts on Monday. I am nervous as hell, but excited all at once. This is going to be great. New friends, new opportunities, and some distance between me and the town that swallows victims whole, only to regurgitate them into working in the local bars and cafes, never to get out again. That sure as hell wasn't my future and I was going to work hard so it wouldn't be.

Grant went to school four hours away. From what I heard, he was having a great time messing around with all the "wrong ones." Apparently, he was enjoying the social side of college, while I hit the books to prove to everyone that I was fully capable of reaching my full potential. I was the perfect combination of book smarts and street smarts. I was going to use this to my full advantage.

The first year of school was a blur. I had some fun, but never strayed too far from my studies. I was trying to make a point. I could do this on my own and succeed.

I went back home on the holidays only to hear that Grant had gone on a fishing or hunting trip and wouldn't be making it back home. For whatever reason this caused my heart to sink just a little more from where it had already sunk the night we were busted. I guess it just wasn't meant to be. The planets were not aligning in our favor and we were like magnets that were polar opposites. We just were not able to be in the same place at the same time. Who knows if it would have even mattered?

The second year of college proved to be more difficult. I needed a distraction and I needed to have a balance between being a student and being a 20 year old that was single in a large city.

Not too long after deciding that I needed a life other than textbooks, I met Craig. Craig was a recently graduated Electrician. He worked for a local company and was out having a great time with friends when we met. He was cute, funny, and flirtatious. He was definitely going to be able to make me shift my focus elsewhere.

Thanks to Craig, Grant became a faded memory. At this time, I didn't know if Grant would ever be anything more. I wanted it so badly, but got shot down. It wasn't going to happen. It was time to put him away in my box of memories. I didn't even know if there were real feelings there. It could have been just my imagination.

As the months passed by, all I could think about was Craig. I was quickly learning how to balance a relationship and school. Craig and I had a lot of fun together. We ended up moving in with each other. Our relationship was moving fast and was wavering on being out of control. We would argue a lot about rent, him flirting with other girls and the possibility of him sleeping with other girls, and of course the topic of why we never had sex always came up. We were not having sex. This was my choice. I was not going to have sex with him when I was constantly wondering if he was with me for the right reasons. Our relationship only lasted for 10 months. It was short but it provided me with the distraction that I was wanting. Craig and I grew far apart and there is no reason keeping someone strung along just to have someone to be with. I enjoyed our time when there weren't other distractions for him, but his left eye was always lazy when it came to beautiful women within close proximity to him. He just couldn't be monogamous when it came to me. Craig and I parted on good terms. He told me that our relationship went from him being completely attracted to me, to being the best of friends and roommates. Shortly after we broke up he met his wife. I guess I was a placeholder for him, so that fate could link him to who he was meant to be with. It just wasn't my time.

After our relationship ended, I would find myself dreaming about Grant. In one dream, I was sitting at a barstool surrounded by his friends. Where was Grant? Just then, the door flew open and in walked a man dressed in a yellow raincoat with the hood up. He lifted off the hood and I was about to run over to him, but it wasn't Grant. It was his friend Carter.

In another dream, Grant kept walking by me. I would reach out to him, to stop him and he would keep walking. It was though I didn't exist. Once again, I would find myself disappointed. Even my subconscious didn't want us together. Why was this happening to me? I broke up with Craig, because it wasn't love. He only wanted me, because he thought he would have this great life with me becoming a vet and him an electrician, he would be able to have money to burn. He never cared about me like I thought he should have. After all, wasn't I a great catch?

Those dreams haunted me. Why was everything so against Grant and I being together? This bothered me enough to take matters into my own hands and call Carter. Carter was home for a little while trying to figure out where his life was taking him and I knew he would have the answers about Grant that I was searching for. Carter and I had been friends throughout school. He would definitely divulge information to me and he wouldn't be breaking any loyalty bond with Grant. I needed his help.

"Carter, this is Savannah." "I know I haven't talked to you in months, and that makes me an awful friend, but I need your help." "Do you know whatever happened to Grant these past couple of years?" "For whatever reason, he popped into my head one day and hasn't left yet." Carter was cool, he knew how I felt about Grant and was always willing to help out where he could. He wanted Grant to break-up with his girlfriend for quite some time, but his persuasion was never good enough. Carter was like an open book. He spilled everything about Grant that has happened in the past two years. He even told me that he was home awaiting the start of his internship. If I was going to have any chance with him, I would need to clear my schedule quickly! So I thought, "why not!" You don't get anything in life that is worth getting without taking a risk and in my mind he was worth it!

This was the opportunity that I had been waiting for. I didn't care if Grant was seeing anyone. Life is short and I was not going to let this go to the grave with me. After all, my mom died young and I wasn't going to risk something happening to me or to him without me telling him how I felt. I would confess my feelings for him and if he didn't feel the same for me at least I manned up and told him. There was nothing to it, but to do it! I packed my things in record time. I threw my bags into the car and prayed that I would get home safely to tell him how I felt. On the way, I ran into a huge rain storm. This almost deterred me from continuing my quest for love. I am not someone that enjoys risking my life that much too possibly get turned down in the end, but this driving force kept pushing me. It was as though I was meant to tell him how I felt and then the universe would change its pull on me. Or would fate change the unwritten story of Grant and Savannah?

Dad was not pleased with my impromptu visit, but I didn't care. I was on a mission and nothing was going to stop me. I was going to give my heart to Grant and then the ball was in his court. He would have to make the decision on what to do with it. Oh God...please let him be home! I drove as fast as I could without getting a speeding ticket. I felt so alive at this time in my life. I was in love and about to tell Grant how I felt. I had feelings for him for quite some time. Now came the time to make them a reality.

Chapter 4

Even though I drove, it felt like I was flying. Like my heart had wings. I never even stopped to think whether or not I was wasting my time. This had to be dealt with now before it was too late. Who knows, maybe it already was. I was going to find out either way. I didn't want too many more years to go by without refreshing his memory on who I was. I didn't want him to forget me. Even though, we had a few times that were special, I needed to make something a little more concrete in his mind.

I called Carter on my way and he said he kept my secret. Grant had no idea that I was coming home. When I pulled into the city limits I swear I went into a heart flutter. Here I was, a success in school, growing up into a young woman, and about ready to fall in love for the first time. I felt so loved just by seeing things that were familiar and seeing people that I had known for years. My heart quickly started to beat normally, but I still felt lightheaded.

I thought my first stop should be my mother's grave. I needed to give myself a pep talk before making myself vulnerable. "Here I am mom." "Maybe I am crazy, but this feels so right." "Can you believe that I am about to do this?" 'If it is meant to be it will be, if not at least I got it off my chest." "Please watch over my heart if it gets broken tonight, make the rejection a little less painful and more bearable." "I wish you were here." I could feel the sun's warmth raining down on me as though she was here with me hugging me. It was just what I needed. Worst thing that can happen is him laughing in my face and telling me to get a life, and then walking out of it forever. I can handle anything that he is going to throw at me. But could I? I wanted the fairytale ending and didn't really stop to think that this could all be in my head. It wasn't. There were too many incidences that would cause me to think differently. I could list them all right now, but it would just cause me to waste precious time.

It's funny to think that after all of these years I still have his parent's phone number memorized. I never had Kyle's number memorized or even Craig's. I guess that is because I had a cell phone and never had to dial it. Or because, I really didn't care to store it in my memory forever.

As I dialed the numbers, my fingers were shaking uncontrollably. I was so nervous. After three rings the answering machine picked up. "Uh…hi this is Savannah. I went to school with Grant. I am home for the weekend and I am wondering if he would be so kind to return my call so we can catch-up." Really Savannah, this is a small town and you were the only Savannah in school, of course they know who you are. Well I guess it was just nerves. What if he is already gone? What if Carter was lying to me, to see how far I would go to make a complete ass of myself? What if he was engaged? Oh my God, I never even thought of that possibility.

The questions just kept flowing through my mind, not helping out the current situation. If I keep this pacing up, Dad is going to want to know what the real reason for my visit is and that he is never going to know. Dad offered to take me to dinner. How the hell could I eat at this time? I was literally sick to my stomach and had no appetite, but I humored him and went with.

After dinner, we drove home. I didn't have much to say other than small talk, because my mind was somewhere else. There was no way I could sit here and wait for someone to call me back. I needed to do my own investigating to find out where he was. I drove past his house and there were no cars that looked like what he used to drive and no lights on in the house. The suspense was killing me. I just wanted to find him.

As I drive through town, I think about what it is that I am going to say to him. I just don't want to cry in front of him. It is so embarrassing, especially if he tells me I am crazy, that then could make me ugly cry and that is just plain ugly. I just don't want to get my heart broken. I know time would heal my broken heart, but I really don't want Grant to be the one to break it. I have never thought of him as being heartless and I really don't know how long it would take to heal if he were to hurt me.

After I drive by all of the places that he might be, I finally drive by Carter's house. It looks as though he is having a get together. One of these cars has to be Grant's. Why is it like trying to find a needle in a haystack? I just want to find him and confess my love to him. Then we can see what the future holds.

I knock on the door and Carter comes running from across the living room floor. "Savannah, its great to see you!" "Is Grant here?" Carter replies with a "Duh, of course he is!" When I turn the corner into the living room, there he is. Wow, he has grown a little facial hair and looks absolutely sexy. I hope he thinks I look good, I have been hitting the gym to help with stress relief. This should help me appeal to his senses.

"Hey Grant, it is so good to see you." He nods in reply. I try to be a little stand-offish to feel him out. All I really want to do is rip his clothes off and get to business, but that would have to wait. Words have to be said first. "So I hear you are headed on an internship?" "Good for you." "It sounds like a great opportunity, when do you leave?" Grant tells me that he is leaving in four days to head to Idaho. And he will be gone for a whole year! Wow, that is extremely far from here and with only four days I had better work fast. This I could handle, I was very good at getting things done in a short amount of time.

I feel as though I am going to need a little liquid courage to help get the words out, so I chug down a few beers and tell him I would love to go and talk somewhere quieter and more private.

We get into his truck and it feels like we are back in a familiar place getting ready to country cruise. With a six pack and the radio turned on, we drive out to where we had our senior party. The night was perfect. The stars were out and there wasn't the usual North Dakota wind. It was still. It was calm, quiet, and offered the perfect setting to get everything off of my chest.

"Grant, does it ever feel weird between us?" "Like there is this unseen connection, and we always seem drawn to each other?" "I have felt it since grade school and I just had this feeling like you would become a special part of my life." "I know this is probably hitting you from left field, but I really need to get this off of my chest or I am going to explode." Grant's eyes look concerned, like he has no idea what it is that I am trying to say or maybe he is scared. Grant allows me to continue. "I mean it is so strange." "I find myself dreaming about you and feel like I need to be with you." "I feel like I had to push through so many hurdles to get to you tonight to tell you this." "I guess what I am trying to tell you, is that I have these feelings for you and I think I am in love with you." I had to stop to catch my breath and wait for his response. This was by far the most vulnerable I had ever been. Oh God.. he isn't saying anything! Way to go Savannah, you go and scare him to death and now he is speechless. He will probably jump in his truck and leave me out here in the dust from his tires. Way to make a complete and total ass of yourself! Grant kind of had a half smile on his face. I couldn't really read him when it was dark and the only light was from his taillights and the moon. "Savannah, I am a little blown away by this, flattered, and speechless." "I have felt that there was something between us and it was easier trying not to read too much into it." "I actually am wondering why it is you telling me this and not me telling you." Grant held my face in his hands and kisses me with the gentlest touch. It felt so right. So I guess this means we are on the same page! He took such care in lowering my back down on his truck bed and sliding me up, so there was room for him. It wasn't the most comfortable place for my first time, but it was with him and it was special. I had waited so long for this moment and took my time. I had to make sure my head and my heart were connecting on all the right levels. It wasn't just some leap of faith, it was more than that. I was in love with him. I deserved to have my chance with him and give him my heart. At this point, we were together. I didn't know what the future was going to hold, but I prayed he was in it with me.

Here we were tangled in each other's arms and in his flannel shirts! The cool breeze blowing over our naked bodies, felt so perfect. After all, North Dakota was where we grew up, and it was where we shared so many memories, it provided the perfect backdrop to making love amongst the wheat and the smell of his cologne.

For the first time, it wasn't like those horror stories that I had read. The articles made it sound like that if you were ever given the opportunity to have it again it would be a miracle, because the first time can be painful. Everything was done with the utmost in care and consideration for making it comfortable. It was what you would want it you were making love with the person that you loved. There was nothing raw about it. It was pure passion.

When we were finished, we laid in each other's arms looking up at the stars covered in a couple of his flannel shirts. I couldn't even talk, I just wanted this moment to never end.

In the next days to come, Grant and I were inseparable. We went horseback riding, fishing, and had more great sexual encounters. We had sex on the dock, in a wheat field, and anywhere else we could go unnoticed for a quickie. It was playful and fun, running in the wheat field and having him chase me, and tackle me only to make love right then and there. Each time it got better and better. After all, our time was limited, and I didn't know when I was going to see him again. The future was not something we could plan out. We needed to sit back and let everything come full circle.

Chapter 5

Today marks the last day of our romantic rendezvous. I didn't want to head back to the city, but school was beckoning me. Grant had a busy time coming up too with the start of his internship. We vowed that we would get together for Christmas and to keep in touch by phone up until the time that we would be reunited. We knew the statistics for long distance relationships weren't good, but we were prepared to go up against all odds. Did we have what it takes? We were prepared to find out.

I left that Sunday so I could make it back to school on Monday. This was the best time I had had In my life. Up until this point, everything else was just okay. I was floating on cloud nine.

The first week back to school was difficult. All I could think about was Grant. I couldn't focus on Anatomy or anything else. The only anatomy I wanted to study was more of Grant's. The weeks turned into months and finally the time came to see Grant again and make our plans for heading back to the place where all of this started.

We talked several times while we were apart. Our schedules clashed, but we found time to talk on the phone from 11 p.m. to 1 a.m. We always could find something to talk about. My phone bill was outrageous. I never complained though, because after all it was my only link to him.

The calendar read December 23rd. Today was the day that he was flying in and we were going to travel back to North Dakota together after we spend the night in a hotel getting reacquainted and tangled in the sheets.

As I sat there trying to think about what to say, I felt myself getting a lump in my throat. I missed him, I loved him, and I wanted us to be able to pick up where we left off.

When I heard his flight get announced that it had arrived safely, my heart was leaping out of my chest. In minutes, I would be in his arms. When I saw him come into view, I had the biggest smile on my face. He was just the way I remembered him three months prior. A couple of his friends were on the same flight as him and were preparing to hop on their next leg of their journey. When their eyes met mine, there was a strange feeling exchanged. I quickly brushed it off when Grant picked me up and swung me around in his arms. This is the place I was longing for. This was a safe place for me. When we walked to my car, we conversed about the next 12 hours stuck in the car and prayed that we wouldn't get stuck in the car in a snow storm. But if we did, we knew how to keep each other warm. When we got to my car, we sat there for what seemed like an eternity, kissing and telling each other how much we missed the other. God, I love this man!

When we got to the hotel, we could hardly contain ourselves. We made it to the room before my pants were at my ankles. He threw me onto the bed and we made love. It was pure bliss. Once again we were limited to the amount of time we had together, so why not get down and dirty right away! Life is short!

I wanted to cherish every moment with him and when we slept I wanted it to be his arms wrapped around me. He was such a part of my life and I wanted him to be for as long as this life would allow it.

This weekend was going to be fun. We would be stepping out together in front of our friends as a couple. I didn't care if anyone had an opinion, because when you love someone nothing else matters. We were not just casual lovers, we were in love. I wanted our friends to be happy for us.

We went to several parties together over the holiday week. We talked about our futures and how both of us had a lot going on. We both wanted to be successful, but also wanted to save room to have someone to share it with. What we needed was a plan to join our two worlds together.

The night that we decided to talk about our futures it was snowing large flakes that were falling all around us. The snow was beautiful and added a touch of romance. The only problem was it was cold, but I wanted to hear everything that he needed to tell me. It was his turn to talk this time. He told me that he wanted to complete his internships, get financially stable, and to find a place to settle with me. He wanted to be able to have something to offer me prior to getting married. I felt the same way, however time was ticking by and you never know what life has in store for you. I was 100% certain that I wanted to spend the rest of my life with him. Grant said that he acted a little off at the airport, because he had a talk with his friends about this and they told him to slow down, even though his heart was racing too. I told him, no matter what I was going to marry him someday. Grant's plan would consist of working hard at his internships, landing a good job, and then settling down. He figured this would take him five years to get enough money to save for a ring and a house once he finished. At the time, five years sounded like a piece of cake. I was in a really great place now and all I wanted was my career and him to share my life with. Five years gave me time to finish school and to start my veterinary practice. I could do this. It was going to be fine.

After our conversation, we went for a snowmobile ride. It was cold, but I had my arms wrapped around his waist and even though I was cold, it didn't matter. He stopped in a low area out of the wind, so we could talk. There was no way we were going to get naked here. If you know anything about a North Dakota winter, it is brutal and we didn't need to have our bodily fluids freeze, sticking us together and being found as "fucking popsicles."

As we sat there and talked, we wondered why it had taken us so long to figure all of this out. Timing was everything. We finished our ride. I went home to my dad's house and he went to his parent's house. I laid in my old bed thinking about him and praying all of this wasn't a dream. Love is so wonderful.

We spent every waking moment together. I didn't want to spend any of my time with anyone else. Our time was limited and he was flying out this afternoon. I felt as though someone had poured salt into my wounded heart and it ached. It was pain that I was feeling, because I was grieving over losing him for however long it was going to be until the next time.

We had two more hours to spend with each other before he had to fly out. I didn't have much to say, because I didn't want him to see me cry. He reached into his pocket and pulled out a little white box. Could this be what I think it is? Of course not, there was no proposal talk at all these last few days and I know it wasn't going to be a promise ring. He opened the box to expose a heart-shaped gold necklace with baguette diamonds. "Here is a little something for you to wear, while we wait to see where we end up." "I love you Savannah." I had already made up my mind that I was going to wait for him. If five years is what it took, I was going to do everything possible to make sure at the end of those five years we would be joined together. I loved him and he loved me. This was not lust, infatuation, or anything else. It was LOVE! He put the necklace on me and I absolutely loved the way the light was hitting the diamonds. It sparkled just like my heart felt, I was so happy.

Chapter 6

Grant left me that December not knowing when we would see each other again. I wore the necklace everyday and when I missed him, I would place the heart in my hand and pray that I would see him soon. The phone calls kept coming and it was enough for now.

I longed to be in his arms and to feel his kiss on my lips. I started saving my money for a plane ticket. March was the month that he had told me would be the best for visiting. I just had to make it through two months and he would be with me again.

January was a long month, but we made it through. February was still hot and heavy until Valentine's Day. He didn't feel like talking on the phone. It had been a long day and he was shot. Before I said goodbye, I wanted to nail down the date that I could come the next month. He could never give me a date.

Something was going on. We just vowed to wait for each other for five years and we have barely made it two months. The statistics were getting the best of us. What had happened in the last few weeks to change his mind? How could we go from hot and heavy to bitterly cold? Did his friends have anything to do with this? Did I do or say something?

These days I found myself to be a little more sensitive. Just thinking about how much I missed him could bring about the tears. This was not normal for me, usually I am fine.

Who was I kidding? We had been careless, actually reckless and I knew what was going on. I could only pass off the nausea and vomiting for so long before one of my friends was going to put two and two together and figure out that indeed there was something growing inside of me. When I looked back on the calendar to count the weeks, I figured I was between 7 and 9 weeks pregnant. I wasn't going to tell anyone and now with Grant being distant I sure as hell wasn't going to tell him. I am not the type to trap him into something and that is what other people would think of this bastard growing inside of me. A trap so that Grant couldn't fulfill his life ambitions, while I would end up not finishing school and probably moving back to Tioga to become what I did not want to be.

With all of the love making and being so clouded by finally being with him, my smarts went directly out the window. I guess at this moment in time I was going to ride it out and see what happened. My mind was swirling around the fact that I wasn't ready to be a mom and the other was saying you are fully capable of pulling it together and being a mom to this baby with or without Grant.

I would find myself looking at websites on pregnancy and abortion. Abortion made me sick. The heart is still beating and they just suck this little fetus right out of you. How insensitive and disgusting! Obviously, this was one of those times that fate and God weren't going to step in and block the sperm that knew right where to swim and the egg that was waiting there like some prostitute on the corner, waiting to get stuck together with what her purpose was.

I had a lot of questions still for Grant and I knew who was going to help me.

The only way I was going to find out the truth or the semi-truth was to call Carter. Carter would know what Grant was thinking, because they were best friends. Carter had to be my ticket to getting answers. I hated this feeling of dread that I was experiencing. It reminded me of the night that my mom didn't come home, and everyone was wondering where she was. Something definitely had been wrong that night and I was getting used to knowing that this feeling meant that there was something not right with the present situation.

"Carter, this is Savannah." "I am borderline desperate for answers and I need you to alleviate this feeling like it is over between Grant and I." My voice was trembling and I was on the verge of a meltdown. "Please tell me what is happening?" "I deserve to know." Carter told me a long winded version of the story about how Grant's boss had a daughter that he wanted Grant to take out. Grant wanted to get hired at this company after his internship and this would be detrimental to him landing the job. Show the boss's daughter a good time, she tells daddy how wonderful Grant is, and Grant gets the job. This was quite a plan and a low blow. Whatever happened to getting a job because you were talented enough to land it? Instead, he was going to date the boss's daughter and work his way up through the ranks. What a plan! I guess she had something that I couldn't offer him and that was money. I came from humble beginnings having to work to get anything that I wanted extra. I had to buy my own car, and pay for my own schooling. This girl knew nothing of what it meant to work hard. Everything was provided for her, even the man that I was meant to be with.

I wanted to burst into tears, but I held it together enough to thank Carter for telling me and I appreciated him breaking the code of silence to give me the truth. Hell, it was more than what Grant was providing me. So this is what a real broken heart feels like. It sucks. I lost him forever.

That night I called Grant and told him I was done talking to him, loving him, and there was no way I was going to wait for him for five years of my life only to be told that he had moved on. He wants to have his cake and eat it too, well so can I. He is not the only man out there that could possibly fall in love with me. That was my first affirmation, but even though it felt good thinking like this, my heart still was broken and I really didn't know if there would be anyone else.

I had to be honest with myself. This was going to hurt and it already hurt bad enough to make me not want to breath, but shrivel up into a blanket and just disappear. This was going to take some time to heal. As I laid there in disbelief, sorrow, and shame, I felt the necklace on my neck. I took it off and threw it across the room. Now the tears were uncontrollable and I was left by myself, only to wonder what had happened. Everything had to have been a lie. I found myself looking into the mirror at the little bump that was appearing on my tight tummy. I didn't spill my little secret to Grant and at this point in time, it was not going to be used as leverage. I hated reading about those girls that would use their babies as a way to keep their men around. I wanted Grant in my life, but not at the cost to my child. Oh my God...did I just call this it, my child? I laid there thinking about what it would be like to have a baby and have to cart the little one to class with me or bring the baby to daycare. It was going to be tough being a single mom, but I knew that this wouldn't have happened to me, if God didn't think I could rise to the occasion and fulfill my duty. I had a little life growing inside of me and now I had to be responsible. I had to turn my moment of irresponsibility into being a grown up and not seeing it as something that was going to ruin my life. Grant wouldn't find out and that was my plan. I know it was a selfish plan, but he had already made up his mind. He was on the verge of forgetting about me and I was never going to be able too.

I planned my first trip to the doctor's office and felt like this would be my first sign of being responsible. Make my well baby check up and make sure everything was okay.

I dreaded all of the questions, like is the baby's dad around? When did you conceive? When was your last period? Do you want to sign up for assistance? My head was about ready to explode and then I heard my name being called. I quickly looked around to make sure no one that I knew was there wondering why I was there. I guess it would be easy to say I was there for my yearly exam, but I looked a little ill to say the least and probably lost some weight from all of the throwing up I had been doing lately.

Dr. Clemens was such a sweet lady. She asked all of the questions I was dreading, but in such a nice way. She didn't pass judgment on me when I said the father was out of the picture and she thought I was being very responsible for deciding to hang on to this little baby and see where life leads us. She asked if I had a support system and I thought well maybe, dad and Jeff would make good fatherly figures for this little one and once the initial shock wears off they just might embrace my decision.

Now was the time I was anxiously waiting for, the ultrasound. I have never had one ever, but couldn't wait to see what the little bundle looked like. As the probe glided over my stomach, I could see something. There it was, just this little human with little arm buds and little legs. The heartbeat was strong and steady. The doctor took measurements and said I was roughly 7 ½ weeks along and that everything looked perfect. I had tears running down my face and wished mom was there to hold my hand and tell me that everything would be fine, but I was alone. I had been alone before at certain milestones and I had gotten use to this. I would be fine and I was going to make a great mother for this baby.

On my way out of the clinic, I thought that just maybe I should be telling someone that I was expecting. I just couldn't decide who I would tell. I thought I would give it some more time, but at some point I was going to start showing and I couldn't blame it on junk food and gaining weight, because I was sulking the loss of my first love.

I thought I should call Jeff. After all, we have been through a lot in our lives and he would be able to keep it a secret until I could muster up the courage to tell dad.

I dialed Jeff's number and then I froze. "Hello Savannah, are you there?" I couldn't say anything so I slammed the phone down. He wasn't the right person I should be telling. I thought about calling one of my aunts. Maybe they could help? Then I remembered how well all the lady figures in my life could keep secrets and knew if I told one of them, they would tell dad. I wanted to be the one that told him, but I was too fragile right now, I couldn't take his gruff attitude.

What about Claire? Or Rebecca? No they would more than likely tell me to remember that advice they had given me back in high school. Don't get pregnant! I couldn't tell them either. I needed to tell a guy, than I could see how they would feel from Grant's perspective. I decided to call Max, my best guy friend. He would be perfect. He would keep my secret and allow me to talk to him without getting a lecture in return.

"Max, I need you!" Oh boy…here come the tears. "I have something to tell you and I am really bad, but I need you to tell me how you would feel it you were in my situation from a male's perspective." "OMG…Savannah, I know what you are going to tell me!" "How far along are you?" Max was a smart cookie and he knew exactly what I was going to tell him before I even got it out. So in between sniffles I told him 7 ½ weeks and the baby is healthy and Grant isn't going to know.

"Bad idea Savannah, it took both of you to create this little bundle of joy and he deserves to know." Max said if he was ever in this situation he would be hurt if he had a baby out there in the world and the mom never told him about it. "Even though I told you the two of you would have ugly children, I am sure everything will turn out just fine and you will have this beautiful baby to show off." "Wow, thanks Max, you always know what to say that makes me feel so much better." "Will you come to the next appointment with me?" "I don't want you to feel like you are going to be stepping into the role of the absent father, but you are the only one that knows and I could really use someone holding my hand." "I am suppose to go back within the next couple of weeks to get some tests done, will you come?" Max hesitated at first, but then he replied with an "of course I will be your support system and be your coach!" That was one thing about Max, I think he grew up with a whistle in his mouth coaching other people. He was an assistant coach when we were in school and now he was going to be my coach for me and my baby. Max was a great friend and confidant. I needed him right now.

I heard the horn honk from the outside of my apartment and knew that Max had arrived to take me to my next appointment with Dr. Clemens. I was nervous, but was told that these were routine tests and I would be able to hear the heart beat again.

"Savannah" there was my name again. Max came with me into the room and he was good comic relief to help ease the nervousness. Max started to play with the Doppler on his own stomach..."nothing!" "I guess I am not pregnant." Dr. Clemens walked in and was surprised to see a man in the room with me. I quickly told her he was not the father, just a friend to support me in my decision to keep the baby. Dr. Clemens was thrilled that I had asked someone to come. She took the Doppler from Max and found the heartbeat right away. It sounded like music to my ears. Max smiled at me and kissed my hand. It was so nice to have him there with me. He provided me with laughs and the ability to calm down and enjoy the time with the doctor listening to the baby. Dr. Clemens didn't need to see me until the first trimester was over, so the next time I would see her I would be showing even more. I decided that after the next visit I would tell people. I had to at some point.

On the car ride home, Max was all smiles razzing me about being Mommy Savannah. I liked hearing it. Even though there was a stigma with being a single unwed mother, I didn't care. Everything happens for a reason and this was going to be my new reality.

Max slammed on the breaks...A car had pulled out in front of us and that's when I felt the impact of the car behind us slamming into us. Max and I jerked forward and the airbags flew out of the dash. I had blood running down my forehead from my head hitting the side window and Max was knocked out. I cried out for help and no one was coming. I heard sirens in the distance, but they seemed so far away.

I let my eyes close and didn't wake up until I was in the emergency room. "Where is Max?" "Is he okay?" No one would answer me. I tried to sit up and the nurses told me to lay back down. I felt a warmth coming from in between my legs and thought maybe I had peed my pants when the impact happened. Then it dawned on me. It wasn't what I first thought it was, it was blood. I sat up and looked down and there it was, blood in the crotch of my pants.

"Nurse, I am bleeding. I am pregnant." The nurse came over to me with this horrible look on her face and I knew then that my baby was no longer going to be apart of my life. I had made all the right decisions, but this accident decided my fate for me.

I lied back done on the gurney and cried like I had never cried before. I felt like this was a horrible nightmare. I never got to make the final decision on what would become of me and my baby, but now it was just me. When I looked on the bedside table there was a little pamphlet about miscarriage sitting there. What a horrible piece of literature. I was not ready to look at it, but then my mind drifted to my best friend Max. Where was he and was he okay?

Just as I started wondering about him, in came a nurse wheeling Max over to the bedside. He was bruised and had a laceration on his left eye. He had been crying too. "Max, are you going to be okay?" Max stood up and kissed my forehead and broke down in tears saying he was sorry over and over again.

It wasn't his fault that I lost my baby. He was being such a good friend coming to my appointment with me and he would continue to be my best friend. I loved my friend Max. Time would heal this wound and my secret would remain safe with the two of us.

I knew how time was the best medicine for the heart that was broken or sad and it would be my lifesaver as time went on.

That night I dreamt about my baby. He was such a beautiful little boy. He had eyes like his father and my round cheeks. He smelled like baby powder and had the most perfect hands and feet. I kissed him and rocked him in the rocking chair and then my mom came and took him from me. I didn't feel like I had to hang onto him, I let her take him from my arms and begged her to keep rocking him and he likes if you sing to him. She smiled at me and took him. She kissed his forehead and put her hand on my cheek.

I felt a lot of comfort from this dream and when I woke up I prayed that I would pull it together and continue on the path that I set out on. I didn't name my baby, but knew that I would carry him in my heart everyday and knew he was in good hands up in heaven with his grandmother. I would see him some day when I too left this world and we would be reunited.

Max's wounds healed and he got a new car. He came over a lot after the accident to check on me and he proved to be my rock. He let me cry on his shoulder and he made me laugh.

Laughter proved to be the best medicine and soon my broken heart was healing. Time was the best gift when it came to dealing with loss. The months went by and I didn't cry like I had in the beginning. I had comfort in my heart and I knew that someday when the time was right I would experience the love of a child and have this extra special love to give in return.

CHAPTER 7

The months went by quite quickly and once again I was wearing a cap and gown graduating from Veterinary School. My whole family came. Dad was so thrilled and proud of me. It only took all of these years! After the last couple of years, I needed to know that I was still someone special in the eyes of another even if it was my dad.

Jeff came too. He was up to his old tricks, flirting with my colleagues. Jeff thought it would be a great idea to go out on the town and celebrate my major accomplishment. At first, I didn't know if this would be beneficial to give me some time to see what was out there, but I deserved to be treated like a Queen tonight and that was exactly what I needed.

I really needed a fun night out, so I could cut loose and forget about the hurt that I still felt. We had a great time. I even met someone. I guess it happens when you least expect it. His name was Aaron. He was a Quarter Horse Breeder on a ranch that he inherited when his father passed away two years ago. We had a lot in common and he was in need of an Equine Vet.

I guess I was just what he was looking for. Aaron was so sweet and kind. He had a gentle look in his eyes and really loved his horses. He wanted me to come and geld some of his studs for him. I obliged, with a little blushing in my cheeks. He was so handsome, kind, and who knows maybe this could really start my career. I looked at this opportunity as a great way to let out some of my pent up frustration with men and what a great way to relieve it by removing a pair of testicles.

In the next couple of weeks, our work relationship progressed into flirtation. Aaron asked if I would like to see him outside of his stables and I was so pleased. I thought he would never ask. He had a lot going for himself, and his dedication to making the best stock was something that I was so impressed by. He had drive and determination, much like my own.

Aaron always shot straight from the hip and told me exactly what his intentions were. He was in it for the right reasons, when it came to his career, and when it came to me. I was as honest with him as possible about how I had my heart broken and I had walls made of concrete surrounding what was left of my heart and he would need a big chisel if he was going to get in at all. I had nothing to give him either. He was successful and I was just starting out with a heaping hill of school debt and the vision of starting my own practice. Aaron was not concerned at all about my worries, he just smiled and said "let's see where this leads us." Life was starting to take a turn from being sad and gloomy, to blooming again. Grant was fading from my memory. At times I was reluctant to allow my heart to move on, because what if there was still a chance? I owed it to myself to try and be happy.

After several months of flirting, and being free of memories, I was ready to take the next step. Aaron wanted me to move in with him. He said his ranch needed a woman around much like me and he was falling in love with me. I guess this was going to happen eventually when I had been spending most of my free time out there with him riding horses, helping him choose stallions to go with his mares. I really enjoyed the time that I spent with him. It was carefree and full of excitement. I told Aaron that I would move in with him, but taking our time was important. I was not ready to rush into being someone's wife, but really wanted to make sure a firm foundation was being constructed out of love and it was mutual.

When I was unpacking my things I found the necklace. I thought I had tucked it away out of sight, out of mind never to be found again, but I was wrong. I held it in my hand and all the memories I tried so hard to repress came flooding back. Grant and the baby were in my mind again. I felt a heaviness in my heart. This time I would pack it away never to be found again. I needed to be free. The heartbreak was one that took longer than I could have imagined to heal and I didn't want to go back there again. Grant probably never even thought about me, so why should I be moping around wondering about him? He didn't know about the baby and that was going to stay that way as long as I had my way.

That October, Aaron and I drove back to North Dakota for him to meet my dad. This was a big step in our relationship and it had to be perfect. I wanted to get dad's seal of approval. I also needed my friends to meet him and give me their honest opinion. I finally had things moving in the right direction.

Once we got there, Dad and Aaron hit it off right away. They made plans for the two of them to go fishing and share "man talk." I stayed behind to find my friends and talk to them without Aaron around. I needed to show them that I was healed and ready to move on. I didn't want Aaron around to hear about Grant. This was my fresh start with Aaron and I wanted to keep it that way.

Claire was the first one that I found. It was so good to see a familiar face and one so special as Claire's. We always got mistaken for sisters. We had such a great time growing up together and vowed that no matter where life took us we would always remain the best of friends. Claire had great stories to tell me about her life in college and how she thought she might have met her future husband. I was so excited for her. Claire deserved to be happy and she had so much love to give that I think this was exactly what I was needing to hear. It was amazing best friends in love at the same time, with men that could potentially be our husbands. Claire and I shared more small talk and then of course she had to turn the conversation onto the one person that I was working so hard at forgetting. Claire warned me that Grant was in town for hunting season. She said they had shared some small talk and she tried very hard to not mention my name. She said he was alone. I dreaded seeing him and prayed that our paths wouldn't cross. Finally, I am in a good place. I made the conscious decision to move on and give this new experience a chance to blossom. The last thing I needed was a flare up of old feelings. Even though I didn't want to see him, I was dying to know if he had mentioned me at all. The curiosity was killing me. Claire said the conversation was no longer than five minutes and there wasn't enough time for her to give him her thoughts on how it ended with me. I was so grateful that she didn't get the opportunity, because knowing her like I do she would have spilled that I was in town for the weekend with my new man and I moved on. Claire wouldn't have left anything out.

When Aaron and dad got back from fishing, I wanted to show Aaron everything that made me who I am, from the school that I attended, to where we use to hang out, and some of the beautiful scenery south of town. I also wanted him to meet two of my best friends, so that I would have a little insight on what they thought of the new man in my life.

After my tour of the area was finished, we met up with Claire and Rebecca. Rebecca was my silly, carefree friend. She found her husband while we were in high school. We would always joke about having a double wedding, because I would be marrying my high school sweetheart and she would be marrying hers. The sad part is she actually did it and well we all knew what happened on my end.

I missed the two of them so much. We all went our separate ways and now here we were again reunited. This was such an exciting time in all of our lives. Claire was getting serious with her man, just like I was with mine, and we had Rebecca to give us marriage advice. Our conversations were long overdue. This was going to prove to be a long night.

We had a handful of bars to choose from and I chose the one that wasn't going to give us lung cancer in the hours that we would spend there reminiscing. As the beers kept coming, Claire and Rebecca grew less nervous and started asking Aaron all sorts of questions. I thought this was great that they were making sure he was the right fit for me. I wanted to see if he wavered in his answers to them at all, but he didn't. Aaron seemed quite amused by their questioning.

Claire, Rebecca, and I got up to leave for the restroom and left Aaron with our guy friend Max. Once we made our way through the crowd of camouflaged hunting parties, we made it to our destination.

"Savannah, it looks like you are moving on quite well with Aaron." "I like him a lot, he is a great match for you." Claire was beaming as she was telling me how great he is and how happy I looked. I thanked Claire for not bringing up my name when she spoke to Grant earlier in the week and she kept it a secret that I was coming to town and that I wouldn't be alone. I am so glad that Grant is staying away from this bar tonight. It really isn't his cup of tea. It is more quaint and less loud then the others. If he showed up, I didn't have the faintest idea what I would say to him. A part of me wants to slap him silly while the other part of me is still in a way heartbroken and wonders if it was all a lie. It wouldn't be long and I would get my chance to find out.

Carter came running up to my friends and I and warned me that Grant came in and he was getting to know Aaron. Carter also said that Grant is a little tipsy and was enjoying his conversation that he was having with Aaron. Grant told Aaron that he was my first love and that my heart still belonged to him. The nerve of him! How dare he try to stir the pot! When we got into the main part of the bar Grant was already sitting back in his barstool avoiding any glare from my eyes. I asked Aaron what was exchanged between the two of them and he told me everything. I could feel the anger growing inside of me. So now he was going to control whether or not I could move on. Last time I checked, he had his chance and he blew it.

This was typical of a guy that thought he had me right where he wanted me. He wanted to have the upper hand and he didn't. After all of these years, he thought by telling my boyfriend that I still loved him would change everything. Granted, Aaron and I were in the early stages of our relationship and it was still vulnerable, but I wanted to make an honest effort of this relationship. I wanted to see if I was capable of moving on and if my heart had healed.

I think it is ironic that Grant was so capable of telling Aaron how I had felt, but what did he feel when we were together, and what in the hell did he feel right now, seeing me with someone else? His strength was never telling me how he felt, but tonight he was speaking for me.

"Grant." I yelled over the loud music. "I want to see you outside now." Grant followed, not quite knowing what to expect. I wanted to kick his ass, kick him in the balls, and punch that smirk right off of his face. "Savannah, you are so pretty when you are mad." Grant said. "Oh don't butter me up you son of a bitch!" "What do you think you are doing?"

"You have no idea what it felt like when you stopped calling, when I was told by someone else that you were dating your boss's daughter." "Did you think I was going to wait for you, while you were exploring someone else's body?" "You must think that I am so stupid." "How dare you play me for a fool!" I was so angry, I thought I was going to bite his head off of his shoulders. "I gave you my heart." "Not just a piece of it, the whole thing." "Those were the best moments in my life." "I don't even feel right telling you this, because all you are going to do is hurt me again." Grant just stared at me not saying anything. "Fucking Coward!" Now he is speechless, well he sure wasn't speechless ten minutes ago. I didn't let anything slip about the loss of our child, because that would change everything. I didn't want his sympathy and I didn't need him to decide he was going to be my knight in shining armor. If he was wanting to be that, he would have to have been it a long time ago.

Grant grabbed my face with force, but he was gentle and planted a passionate kiss right there on my lips as though they remembered where they had been so long before. I was trying so hard to not kiss him back. "Stay Strong!" It was no use, I was putty in his hands. I was suffering from paralysis. I couldn't move. My heart melted with his touch. The feelings for him came flowing back at full force. "Look me in the eye and tell me you don't feel anything." Grant was dead serious, he wanted to know if my heart still belonged to him. My heart said to scream that I loved him and I still wanted him, but just as I was about to open my mouth Aaron and the girls walked out. They were concerned that they would find Grant a dead man lying on the sidewalk, but instead they caught us in a special moment, still in an embrace. It was obvious that I wasn't kicking his ass. It was also obvious that they had walked in on more than just a hug. Aaron looked confused with hurt in his eyes and that crushed me. I walked away from Grant and told everyone it was time for us to head home. I really should have told him about the baby, but did he have a right to know?

Aaron and I were together now and this whole baby topic would be something that would need to be explained to the both of them and I just didn't have it in me right now. In a way, I wanted Grant to feel loss too, like I had. Thank God for Max. He was there for me when I needed him and now Aaron was allowing me to heal my broken heart by slowly forgetting about Grant. Up until now, I had done a great job. This night would go down in the memory books as being the night that I should have told Grant and the night that I should not have been so stubborn and just told Grant that he still had my heart, but mum was the word.

Max's eyes met mine and he knew that I didn't say anything about the baby. I think in the back of his mind he thought that I should have, but he didn't pressure me. He knew that in time the truth would come out and until then the ball was in my playing field. The best thing about Max is, he could read my mind. I just looked at him and he knew the answer. Max also knew how the truth would probably jeopardize my relationship with Aaron.

Aaron and I were leaving in the morning and we needed to get our rest. It was a long drive and we needed to be prepared for it.

So was his kiss his way of telling me he still had feelings for me? I never got closure. Aaron and I left the next day. The drive was long and I felt like I needed to explain what Aaron saw. I told him yes indeed Grant had my heart at one point, but moved on and thought I would still be waiting for him like some fool. And for as stupid as I was, Grant still had half of my heart and Aaron had the other. It was just the way it was going to be until I could get Grant's memory out of my heart and mind forever. I didn't know how long it would take and I didn't know if I truly wanted it gone. It was all so confusing. I wanted to be able to say that only one man occupied my heart, but it wasn't true. I loved them both. I guess the real question was, did Grant love me? Or was it pure jealousy that came over him that night? Why couldn't he have just used his words instead of his lips? All he did was add more confusion into the mix, something that I didn't need to complicate everything.

I knew that once we returned home Aaron was going to make it official. He had gotten my Dad's approval along with everyone else and it would be only a matter of time until he proposed. Was happily ever after in the cards for me? I guess this was something I had to determine for myself. I didn't even know if I was ready for this?

When I looked back at my life, it made me have this overwhelming feeling like it was time to settle down with someone, have a couple of kids and just "be". Be what? Housewife? Boring? This was not me, I could be a housewife and not be boring. After all, Aaron loved me for me. He didn't seem to care if I gained ten pounds and looked a little fluffy, or if I had bad morning breathe. For some reason, Aaron was in love with the ugly me, the fat me, the no make-up me, and me.

Aaron made me feel like a Goddess. He was prepared to give me everything that I deserved. He and I had so much fun together, constantly laughing and making the other the butt of our jokes. He was never going to ask me to wait for him and he surely wasn't going to not tell me what his heart was telling him. He wore his heart on his sleeve and that is something that I appreciated so much. I knew how he felt about me from day one. I owed it to myself to be happy now. I had to stop thinking about all of this Grant stuff and finally move on.

That night I dreamt about Grant. I dreamt how life would have been so different if he didn't make up such dumb rules and if he would have told me it was time for me to be with him. I would have. I was so in love with him. I dreamt that we were out in the wheat field just holding each other. It was peaceful. Then it was time to kiss, and his lips vanished along with the rest of him, like he was something that no longer existed. I yelled at him "come back to me!" He was nowhere to be found. Then I woke up. This was a nightmare. It was unfinished business to come back and haunt me. He officially became my "what if." This was the one thing I never wanted in my life, unfinished business, something that would just linger waiting to fester at the wrong time. I had no closure. I never got the last word in and he never used any. I was sick to my

stomach all day. I couldn't eat, because I just wanted answers.
"If only he would have said that he loved me."

   After the nausea finally left and the lump in my throat
dissolved, I felt this overwhelming anger once again. This time
it was because he was a son-of-a-bitch. Actually he wasn't a
SOB. I really liked his mother and she would have been an
amazing mother-in-law. And she would have been a great...well
I couldn't even say the word. He was just a disappointment. It
was fate's way of saying this just wasn't going to be and at this
time in my life I had to realize it the hard way. I couldn't have
his baby and I couldn't have him. It was time to move on.

CHAPTER 8

Aaron proposed to me at his Quarter Horse Booth at the Horse Expo. I guess this was his way of being romantic. Horses brought us together as well as the drink that I bought him the night we met.

The proposal was sweet. Everyone clapped and told me how lucky I was. He is a great catch! This was my chance to officially move on. I had to give myself a pep talk about the whole, this is what is meant to be, now suck it up and smile, show your ring off, and start planning the wedding. The next chapter in my life was starting, and I needed to buckle up and enjoy the ride.

Aaron and I shared the news with our family and friends. Jeff was thrilled, because he was going to be in the wedding and be able to hit on my cute bridesmaids. Dad already knew that it was going to happen, thanks to Aaron being a gentleman. And my friends were happy, yet reserved, because they knew that I always dreamed that Grant and I would be walking down the aisle together as husband and wife. I had to tell Claire, that sometimes this is just how life throws the ball at us and I caught it. Aaron loves me!

The necklace was hidden in a spot that I would never think of finding it. I couldn't find it in a time like this, because I made my mind up already. I was going to be Aaron's wife and that damn necklace would only bring up feelings that needed to allow dust to cover them. Aaron deserved my complete attention, not to mention my whole heart.

We had a long engagement, because I wanted everything to be perfect. I had dreamt of this day since I was a little girl. I was getting this wonderful man and my dreams were coming true.

Our wedding day was beautiful. I didn't want it to be overkill, so we picked a spot on the farm and decorated it with white roses, and kept the rest simple. Our family and friends attended and everyone gave us their blessing. It was a day of joy, but there was plenty of sadness too. It was obvious that two people very dear to us, were not there to share our special day. And neither was my son. The something blue at the wedding was a little piece of a blue outfit the baby would have had. It was so special to me and when people asked, I had said I just loved this color of blue and it made me smile. I put a little baby powder on the piece of cloth too, but that would be my little secret. Even though he wasn't here with me, I knew he was still a part of me.

Aaron was missing his dad and of course I was missing my mom. I hope that she would be happy with the decision that I made.

After the wedding was over, I knew that the big farmhouse wouldn't stay quiet for long. Aaron wanted a son and it was going to happen soon after we celebrated our wedding night. I guess this is what you do once you get married. You start popping out babies faster than you could ever imagine, because heaven forbid you wait until you are older and your body doesn't bounce back. I was ready to hold a baby in my arms and prayed that it wouldn't take long to get pregnant. I wanted to have something to hold this time and I vowed to be extra careful.

Griffin came into our lives in the Spring along with five colts. He was the apple of Aaron's eye and of course his father's namesake. He looked like his daddy, but always had a soft spot for his mother. When I looked in to his little eyes, all I wanted was to love him and show him the right way to go about things in his life. He would inherit this farm when we decided we no longer wanted it and he would eventually marry and have kids of his own. I wanted to make sure when he was old enough to know that you "say what you mean and mean what you say." He was going to know how to finish the business that he starts in his life.

I had several years to teach him how to be a good man and an honest man. He was going to make me proud someday, I could just feel it.

A year after Griffin came into our lives, we welcomed a little girl named Scarlet. She was named after Scarlet in "Gone with the Wind." I loved that movie, but much like life it doesn't necessarily end the way I would have wanted it too. Here I was a mother of two, not even 30 years old yet. This is how I wanted it to be. I wanted to be young and vibrant and have energy to chase my kids and still be young enough when they grew up.

The things I wanted for Scarlet were different from Griffin. I wanted her to be a strong woman and to never lose her voice. To stay strong when life hands her challenges and to love with all of her heart even if it gets broken. If her heart was to ever break I was going to make sure I did everything in my power to catch it and put it back together for her. I wanted to protect her heart from guys like Grant, but then I wanted her to experience even the kind of love that didn't last. I want her to love herself and to never give up.

I was so busy being a mother, that Grant finally was just a memory with a thick layer of dust. I never thought about him again after my daughter was born and that was fine with me. I never even heard his name mentioned when my family would go home for the holidays. Finally, I was free for the first time in years.

Life continued and the past stayed where it was meant to be, but of course when you let your guard down something happens to bring it back into full focus.

Here I was doing the books for my business and working on the sales and stud fees for Aaron when "you've got mail" flashed across the screen. I was a little annoyed and clicked on it to make it disappear. I would come back to it later.

Finally the suspense was killing me. Just before I clicked on it, it was though my mind already knew who it was from. Apparently, the part of me that I had thought got rid of that memory just kept it buried for a little while. Right then, my mind yelled "Grant." I knew it was something from him. There it was in front of me on the screen. He sent me an e-mail. What the hell could this possibly be?

Dear God in Heaven, you just couldn't keep him away from me, could you? There it was, To: Savannah, From: Grant. No Subject. What could he possibly have to say to me after all of these years.?

"Savannah, five years have passed if you haven't noticed and I am writing to tell you that I am getting married next month. Are you happy?" Grant

So it has been five years. He was right. Did he think that I could actually be that patient to wait for him? Patience is a virtue, but not one that I practice. Obviously, I moved on just fine, look at my life. I am a mother of two wonderful kids and a wife to the best husband around. Apparently, he was the one that was still thinking of me or his arrogance was getting the best of him. Maybe the boss's daughter was his ticket to success and now he was ready to have a wife like me in his life. Or maybe, better yet, he grew a conscience? Could that even be possible? Maybe the kiss that never got finished haunted him like it had haunted me. I guess I would never know. I had to write back, to let him know I was happy.

"Grant, I am flattered by your e-mail, however I have two kids and I am still married to Aaron. I love my family very much. You should have told me how you felt on the sidewalk after you kissed me. I felt something for you that was what I have always felt. I guess you are too late." Savannah

I sat there staring at the screen for what seemed like an eternity before I hit send. Why is there a tear falling down my cheek? Oh my God, I am crying over him again. This should not be happening. I pretended in my heart that I was okay with him getting married to this girl that had what was rightfully mine so many years ago. It wasn't true. I tried to be happy for him, but all I wanted was a stiff drink and a bubble bath.

I called Claire to tell her and she was shocked. She couldn't believe that he would e-mail me all of these years. Why didn't he just call, it would have been nice to hear his voice one last time. That night after getting buzzed off of red wine in the bubble bath, I vowed that it was over. No more dreaming of him or thinking about him. Fate didn't want us together and so it was time to put it to rest.

CHAPTER 9

Life continued after that moment in the Fall. The leaves coming off of the trees were like my memories of the times we had together shriveling up and dying. It was symbolic, yet heartbreaking.

Aaron and I hit a bad streak in our marriage. The horse market plummeted and no one was buying horses for what we were selling them for. We were going broke except for my vet practice. Lately, I was putting animals down, because they were ill and no one wanted to take the time to nurse them back to health. It was sad. Our farm couldn't become a sanctuary for all the unwanted horses, so I had to do what I was sent out to do, get rid of the ones that no one could afford to feed or break.

This took a toll on my attitude towards life. You just don't throw away something that you no longer want when a beating heart is involved. I felt so strongly about it when it came to all of the horses, but then to watch the news and see a teenage girl throwing away her baby, this just made it worse. What is wrong with people?

After my long day of ending horse's lives, all I wanted to do was go home and take a bath. The kids were gone for the night, so it would be just Aaron and I. It was already past dark when I pulled into the drive. When I rounded the corner, there was a car that didn't belong. I was shocked to see that Aaron had someone over being in the foul mood he was in lately.

No lights were on in the house, but the barn was well lit. I thought it was strange to have someone out at this hour looking at the stallions, so I thought I would meander down to the barn and see what was happening. When I got there, I saw something that would stay in my mind forever. Aaron was tangled in a saddle blanket with this woman I had never seen before. They were having sex on the hay oblivious to me standing there. So this is how betrayal feels. I looked for something to grab to throw at them and the only thing next to me was a pitchfork. For as much as I wanted to kill him and her, I thought I would choose the less dangerous choice and scream "What the fuck are you doing?" They both startled when they heard me and Aaron of course looked like he was going to have a heart attack. This time he was busted, Lord knows this wasn't his first time. We had been having a difficult

91

time and now here we are looking at it dead in the eyes. I didn't care that he was having an affair with another horse breeder. As far as I was concerned they could go fuck each other anytime they wanted, because I was taking the kids and we were leaving the farm.

Aaron got dressed and followed me to the house. His lady friend left in a cloud of dust after I told her to leave before I killed her. That was all it took and the whore was gone. Aaron on the other hand, looked a little scared for his life. I wasn't going to hurt him. He wasn't worth my time. I just felt stupid that I let my intuition get muffled to the point that I had to change my focus to not think about what I had already known to be true. Dumb! That is all that came to mind. I was dumb. We hadn't had sex in a month, and when we did touch prior to that it was loveless. He didn't have that spark in his eye and it felt like we were strangers screwing just because we could.

He didn't love me anymore, but he didn't want to end it for the convenience of keeping the kids in one place. I was better than this. He was a weak man that let his own failures get the best of him. If only he knew we were a team. When one failed the other carried them, so that no matter what the team stayed strong. This was not our case. I would have carried him until my knees buckled underneath me, but he didn't have that kind of dedication. It was a "man thing." It was about him having to rely on a woman to lead the way and he couldn't deal with it, so he found a whore in a bar that made him feel like a man, because after all she was a waitress. This was the second time that he fucked me over. She could never help him financially. Therefore he never would feel like he was having to bow to a woman. It was all pathetic and cowardly. Once again my heart was broken, but this time only the portion that he was able to occupy. He didn't have all my heart like I had tried to make myself believe.

We had kids together, but that was the only thing we would be sharing. I was going to drop him like yesterdays trash and pick up my things and start over. I was not one to sulk this time. I had a great business and I had kids to stay strong for. Shame on him! Now he made my job in raising a kind, thoughtful, faithful, young man even harder. I was going to work extra hard so that when Griffin started dating he would fear my hemostats and scalpels, because if he ever hurt a girl like his daddy hurt me, he would end up without his testicles.

CHAPTER 10

My class reunion was coming up in the summer time and I was going to go as a free agent. My divorce was final in May and I had two months to get rid of the dark circles under my eyes and start looking like one hot mama that had a lot to offer someone, well maybe just a good roll in the hay! I guess that is what the new trend is these days.

I wasn't looking to find my knight in shining armor, because the only one that I wanted from my graduating class was married. I was not going to sink to the same level that Aaron did. Marriage is sacred and deserves to be treated as such. I just wanted to see if the possibility presented itself under certain circumstances. I just might get to relive my past with Grant.

The reunion came and went. It was a lot of fun. Grant never showed up. There was a certain amount of curiosity about what ever happened to him and if he was still married.

It was great catching up with old friends and being back in my old stomping grounds. I missed my home town, but I missed seeing my dad even more. This town has always been home. It will always be the place that I can come home too and bring back fond memories of growing up and visiting with people that helped raise me.

When my friend Max brought up Grant, I know he could see the sadness in my eyes. Here I was finally all alone and in a really good place, he on the other hand was nowhere to be seen. Max tried to make me feel better by telling me it's a good thing Grant and I never got married and had kid. He probably would have hurt me in the end anyways.

There is a reason to why we were never given the chance to rekindle our love affair and the only reasoning behind it is that his pursuit of me was never more than a dream. It was a fairytale and this time the princess didn't get her prince. It will remain one of life's many mysteries.

We went our separate ways and that is all there is left to say about it. I hate seeing or hearing his name. The ache comes back and it presents itself like the plague. It takes awhile to let the memory fade. It's like smoke clearing from a fire after it has been put out with water. At times it lingers longer depending on what is happening at the time. Especially, if I am driving back to North Dakota and pass a wheat field. I see us dancing in the field with his arms around me. It was such a safe and happy place. We would spin around until we got dizzy, just to wind up making love in the wheat. He would look right into my eyes with such care and pick the wheat out of my hair. I blink my eyes, because now they are clouded by tears. I don't want to cry over him anymore, but if he were to stand in front of me and tell me that he loves me, we wouldn't be standing for long. He was my first true love. Not to mention, I would have to tell him about the son we had together that never got to take his first breathe. I wonder if he would be hurt like I was when it happened?

I hate fairytales. They give young girls the false hope that when they do fall in love it is going to last forever. Love is not guaranteed. Love may even have an expiration date on it. Love can hurt, and love can make you soar. I had all of the above when it came to my time with Grant. I soared and I crashed and burned.

One gloomy Sunday, I was laying around with a fire going in the fireplace and a cup of hot chocolate. It was just a lazy day. The kids were with Aaron and I was having a moment alone. I don't remember dozing off. The phone rang breaking my silent vacation. I looked on the caller I.D. and it was Claire. Just what I needed was a call from my best friend to make the gloom go away.

When I answered the phone her voice was shaking. "Savannah, I have terrible news." "Grant and his wife were in a horrible car accident, she died and he is on a breathing machine." "It doesn't look good for him." "Maybe this is the time that you come and get it off of your chest and let him know that you are still in love with him." I was mortified. I couldn't even say a word. Come hell or high water I couldn't hear that he was dead. I got all of the information about his hospital, the room, and visiting hours. I had to get to him before it was too late.

Once again, I was in my car in record time driving back to North Dakota to be there for my friend, my past lover in a time of need. I couldn't let him die without knowing that I still had a place for him reserved in my heart. I loved him still. Even though we went our separate ways he was the one for me. I didn't think about his prognosis once he got out of the hospital if he did. I just wanted to get this off of my chest again. I felt like every minute that went by was one less minute that I would have with him. It was a 12 hour drive. I should have flown home, but of course there are no flights when you need them.

I pulled over for gas and as it was filling up my dry tank, I thought to myself "am I really suppose to be doing this?" He is going to be full of sorrow and here I am coming in to take the hurt away from him. But I couldn't let him die alone. I am sure his mom would be there and she would be okay with me coming, but would anyone else be okay with it. And I guess the other question was, do I care? Of course I cared about him, hell I loved him. At one time in my life, he is all I thought about. He was the father of our unborn child and this connection that we have always had pulled me to North Dakota like none other than I have ever felt. Was fate finally letting me get what I deserved? Grant was always the one, but then it hit me. Here I am driving in the car, coming to see him. This was the second time. The first time was great I was elated and this time I was trying to beat the grim reaper. Should I be the one traveling for him? Where was the chase when it came to him?

CHAPTER 11

I got to the hospital in record time. Thank God my dad still has friends on the police force and I was able to talk myself out of two tickets. I told them I had to get to the hospital, because someone needed me. Grant didn't know it, but I was a couple of steps away from holding his hand and telling him that he couldn't leave me without knowing that I still loved him.

I made it to the ICU only to find the bed he was suppose to be in empty. I was too late. I walked back into the hall about ready to fall to pieces when I seen his mom at the nurse's desk. She had a bag in her hands, probably his belongings. I didn't want to go over there to have her confirm my greatest fear, but I had too. I needed closure now.

I walked over to her and she was surprised to see me. I gave her a hug and she said that "Grant would be so pleased to know that you came all this way." So this was it, now she is going to tell me that he is dead. "Savannah, he was downgraded this morning. He is off the ventilator and he will be here for a few more days on observation, but you can see him." My heart fell to the ground. I almost became lightheaded, but now I found myself running to his room. I came into his room with a little more grace then I was showing from running down the hallway like someone had called a "code blue". His eyes were closed and bruised, but he was able to squint to see me. "Savannah, is that you?" "Am I dreaming?" "No Grant, you are not dreaming, I am here." I kissed him on his forehead and told him there is not one place I would rather be on this earth than right here with him at this moment. I told him I was sorry to hear about his wife and he informed me that they were on their way home from telling his parents that they were getting a divorce. She was not okay with it and grabbed the wheel steering them into oncoming traffic. He was able to correct the car, but another car slammed into his wife's side of the car killing her instantly. He was very much grieving, but there was no love there anymore. As he talked he got really quiet and drifted off to sleep. I stayed with him until he woke up again. He had me pinch him, so he knew he wasn't dreaming. I told him my marriage was over too and that I had never had any luck dating anyone when my heart still belonged to him.

I couldn't believe that this was how we were going to get our second chance. He was laid up in a hospital bed as a widow and I was a divorcee that had two kids and lived 12 hours away. He was going to need rehab to get him to walk again after he broke both of his legs and he was going to be out of work for quite some time. I let him know that I would be there for him, if he wanted me to be. He assured me that he wasn't going to let me slip away from him again.

I had to get back to my practice and he had to get better. We vowed to stay in touch better than we had before and we did. I looked into moving my practice to North Dakota and checking on whether or not Aaron and I could share custody across state lines.

Aaron had remarried and didn't have time for our two kids, because he had a new baby of his own with his new wife. I gained full custody of our children and moved back to North Dakota.

I never thought in a million years I would be back to where it all began. Sometimes life takes you in different directions only to have you return to where it all started.

Grant made a full recovery and we started out slow. He was grieving the death of his wife, because at one time there was history and love. I let him have his time and was there for him when I was asked.

He assured me that all he needed was some time to figure out his next move and this time I understood that time was okay. After all, I had grieved the end of my marriage too and I was not ready to start anything right away. I told him about our baby and he cried. It was something I could no longer keep from him, especially when he had almost died himself.

That is when I woke up... It was all a dream. That was one crazy dream. Was my mind trying to tell me that I had kept a secret too long and that if something happened to him, he would never know that we had a son that died when Max and I were rear-ended by that distracted driver so many years ago. But did he need to know? Wouldn't that cause issues for him and his wife or would it just be closure. I have carried this secret for years and then I would be free of it and he could do whatever he wanted with the news.

This dream was a haunting reminder of not getting things off of my chest and having it come up when I least expected it too.

What if I told him about our baby? Would it change anything? Probably not.

CHAPTER 12

Grant wasn't going to find out about the baby. I didn't want to be one of those people bringing up old issues from the past only to have him tell me I was crazy and would do anything to get him back even if it was making a story up about our dead baby. I didn't want to break up his marriage and figured that if he was to be married to her than that is how his story would end. He would be this married man, and have kids with her and he would get to see his eyes looking back at him and I wouldn't get to see that ever.

I dreamt a lot about our baby at different stages in his life. When he would start walking, talking, his first tooth, and what he would look like as he grew older. I didn't think I was living in the past, but it gave me a little comfort to feel like I was with him in my dreams.

What if he would have survived the crash? I think we would have been fine. I would be a mother of three and he would have been the older brother. He might have even had a relationship with Grant.

As I was lost in my "what if", the doorbell rang. Was I expecting anyone? This time my eyes were opened and I knew I wasn't dreaming.

I went to answer the door and to my shock Max was standing there with flowers and a bottle of wine.

This was an interesting turn of events. Max and I had always talked and stayed in touch after our class reunion. He had moved to the area to start teaching at the local university and coaching basketball. It was so nice to have someone that knew me from so long ago, being here in the same city. I didn't have to explain to him that I like these certain things, or have to explain anything about my past or where I have been in life, because he already knew all of that.

Max never judged me for the decisions I have made in my life and he has always been my greatest support, besides Jeff.

Things came so naturally with Max and he was so much fun to be around. He knew about my divorce and he loved to play with the kids. He taught Griffin how to play basketball and Griffin was getting really good at it. Scarlet liked how funny he was and he was always making her laugh, much like he would do to me when we were younger.

He was my best friend and now here he was with flowers and wine. What was the occasion? Max just smiled and said "I realized the day and it's your birthday beautiful." "You can't be all alone on your birthday!" I guess with everything that has gone on over the past year, I never even noticed the months passing by and that yes indeed it was my birthday.

Max poured two glasses of wine and we sat by the fire. It wasn't anything weird that we would sit snuggled up to each other, because we were friends. I was so comfortable with him and he was comfortable with me, so it all just worked.

I have never kissed him and had those types of feelings for him, but I was lonely. I was missing the companionship of a man in my life and Max just fit right now. I wanted to feel a man's arms around me again and the warmth of two bodies touching. Max and I were fully clothed, so there was nothing like that going on right now.

Max and I shared a lot of fond memories with each other and it was nice to have some grown up conversation. My birthday has always been a day that I like to do something special for myself, but this year I had forgotten and Max helped to fill that void. Thanks to him, I received beautiful roses and a wonderful bottle of sweet red wine.

We ended up finishing the bottle that he brought and I opened one that I had in my wine cabinet. We ended up getting a little tipsy off of the wine and I told him he wasn't going to drive home. I didn't need him to be in another accident.

I made the couch into a bed for him and tucked him in as though he was my grown child. I kissed him on the forehead and told him "goodnight." I went up the stairs to my bedroom and pulled the covers back and climbed into a big bed all alone.

I just fell asleep when I heard the door creak open. I thought it would be the kids, but then quickly remembered they were with their dad tonight. Someone was coming into my room and I still pretended to be asleep.

I felt the covers open just enough for this person to sneak in. It was a grown man, Max? Max snuck into my room and now was coming into my bed. I felt his arm come over my body and pull me closer to him. I opened my eyes and he kissed my lips. I kissed him back. It was a little weird to be kissing my best friend, but after all we had a history together too and he knew all of my secrets.

Now he was giving me an x rated birthday present. And there was no way I was going to tell him no. I was a lonely divorced woman with two kids and hadn't even started dating that much and now I was going to be with a man that I have known all of my life. I was going to let it happen and in the morning we would determine if it was too weird or not. Maybe it was just the wine?

I tried to be responsible this time. I told him I wasn't on anything to prevent a pregnancy, but he didn't stop. Actually, he didn't seem to care.

Max and I laid there in each other's arms and fell asleep. When I woke up in the morning he wasn't in bed with me. He must have been able to sneak out just like he had snuck in. Quickly and quietly! I was quite hung over from the bottles of wine that we drank, so I was not surprised that he was gone. I wasn't going to notice if a truck came barreling into my room right now.

When I started to wake up more, I could smell something coming from downstairs. It smelled like bacon and eggs. So not only does he surprise me on my birthday with several surprises, but instead of sneaking out and leaving me to wonder what the hell happened last night he stays and makes me breakfast! Okay...this is okay, right?

I really hope it isn't weird when we see each other. I grabbed my robe and headed downstairs to try and choke down the breakfast and find some much needed Advil.

When I seen Max he was standing in my kitchen in just his boxers. He was so cute. His dark hair and dark eyes just smiled with delight. He was very proud of his fried eggs and bacon and never even complained of having a headache.

I accused him of being sneaky and he just smiled and said "what you didn't like it?" "Gee, you gave me the impression that things were coming along just fine." He was always the funny one, full of surprises with plenty of smartass comments to follow.

I just smiled at him. Actually I think I was glowing. We ate breakfast as though we had been married for years and talked as though nothing out of the ordinary happened last night. It was a strange kind of weird, but I guess it was meant to be.

We had a lot to talk about, because this changed everything between us, not too mention the lack of birth control. What if I were to get pregnant with his baby? Then what? Max just took everything in stride. He didn't care. He joked about us be sinners and how dare we have premarital sex. Who would believe that we would be doing the nasty with each other? Everyone that we knew would never believe us.

I guess this was something that made the whole story funny. Max and Savannah are a couple? Who would have thought that this would be possible?

Max told me that if we were to continue, no more thinking of that loser Grant and that he would make the most of being someone that the kids could trust and would love to become a part of their lives.

All the hard work in a relationship was gone, there was none. We already knew everything there was to know about the other and that made it very easy.

Max and I were falling in love with each other and the funny thing we already loved each other as friends, now we loved each other, because we just did!

Max took his new role with great ease. The kids loved him and loved that I had smiles on my face on a daily basis. Max made me so happy, and it was still the honeymoon phase. I wondered what would happen as the years progressed and we turned into an old couple.

Max and I dated for several months and the fun always was present. Aaron enjoyed coming to pick the kids up, because even the kids had different attitudes and we were able to put our differences aside and co-parent the kids. Aaron was happy for us and it was nice to have his blessing.

I was a little gun-shy of the whole topic of marriage. I didn't know if it was something that I should do again, but with Max it seemed like something that should be done. Max wanted to have kids of his own and wanted to have me as his wife.

Max and I went on a much needed get away to the Bahamas. The kids were furious that they didn't get to go, but sometimes adults need to have fun without having to parent all of the time.

I was lying on my beach towel soaking up the rays when I noticed Max was writing in the sand with a stick. The waves would come rushing in, he would curse and have to start all over. I thought it was quite amusing.

When he was finally done he said "Savannah look at my words!" A big wave washed over his words just as he said it and what was left was like a fill in the blank word puzzle.

Max said "I know you are smart and can figure it out." "Max, how about you say it, say the words that are not completely washed away." " I want to hear it from you!"

Max stood up and yelled "Savannah, will you be so kind to make me the happiest man in this world and marry me, so I will never have to be alone ever again?"

"Oh...is that what you were trying to put in the sand?" "Well that was very creative." "Well Max, I guess it is only a given that we have had such fun together over the past couple of months, and you have always been such a great friend to me, and my kids love you and it seems like an alright thing to do." "Jesus, Savannah just say the word!" Max was just hanging on every word that I was making him wait for.

"Well then, Yes!" "Yes, Max I will love to make you the happiest man on the face of this Earth and it would be my honor to be your wife."

Well this was going to be the start of another chapter in my life. I was going to marry my best friend and just maybe we would find happiness that would last a lifetime.

Our vacation was cut short, because we were thrilled of our news that we felt like we needed to share to people in person as soon as possible.

The kids were so happy and told Max that it was about time he sucked it up and asked me. The funny thing is Max asked the kids what they had thought of his plan to ask me on our vacation and he ended up getting a thumbs up from both of them.

All of our mutual friends from school were shocked at first and then gave us their blessing. We planned to head back to North Dakota for the wedding, so everyone would be able to attend. It wasn't going to be anything huge. It was going to be simple, because that is how Max and I both were.

We planned to have a summer wedding, so we knew the weather would cooperate and we wouldn't be worrying about snow in October or cold weather in April.

Chapter 13

We had the car packed to the top as we drove back to North Dakota for our wedding. The kids were going to be a part of this big day and it was going to be a celebration of love and family.

Max's mom was crying the whole time and was so happy that he finally mustered up enough courage to ask me to marry him. She wanted a lot of grandchildren and she wanted them soon.

Aaron gave me a huge hug before we left and was happy that I was finally going to get my fairytale ending. He said he always liked Max and seeing our kids happy was something that was priceless. He apologized for not being able to give me the happy ending that I deserved and said that he hoped that life would always give Max and I what we would be blessed to have. I thought it was a nice gesture and returned the hug with a kiss on his cheek. It was kind of weird that we were now friends and no longer lovers, but parents to two of the sweetest most well behaved kids around.

Our friends showed up, because I think a part of them thought that maybe Max and I were high and we were pulling a practical joke on them. But as soon as they seen the flowers and everyone dressed up, they quickly seen that this was real.

I wore a simple ivory dress that came just below my knees. It was classy for my second wedding and made me feel gorgeous. My hair was simple and had a flower placed next to my French twist. No veil for Max to mess with. Simple was a good thing. Scarlet wore a cute light pink dress and had ringlets in her long blonde hair, and Griffin wore a suit. He looked very distinguished. He walked me down the aisle to my future.

Max and I wrote our vows and they were the most heartfelt words I had ever had spoken to me. Max said that he was so fortunate to have me and two kids that he would call his own. It was the perfect day. We were surrounded by people that loved us and we were in love for all of the right reasons.

A dance floor was assembled in my dad's backyard with a tent to house all of the people. A champagne fountain sparkled in the corner with a picture perfect tiered wedding cake.

We danced our first dance as husband and wife and it was to one of my favorite songs. The words of the song echoed our new found love and life together. This was the start of our future together and it was only going to grow from here.

I was standing alone just taking it all in when I felt a tap on my shoulder. I turned around and to my amazement Grant was standing in front of me. He smiled and had kind of a baffled look on his face. Like he couldn't believe I married Max.

"Savannah, you took my breathe away." "You look amazing." "I was in town and had heard some interesting news about a wedding happening over here at your dad's place and thought he finally tied the knot, only to hear that it was you and Max?" "When did this all happen?" I didn't think he deserved to hear about how Max and I fell in love, because now here I was once again being swept off of my feet and it was by someone that wasn't him.

"Well, I am sure you are surprised, but I guess when things are meant to happen they just do." That was the best I could come up with. He then went on to tell me that he had heard a rumor over a year ago about a baby that was lost in a car accident and who the two people were that were in a car wreck. He apologized for the loss of mine and Max's baby. Who told him that there was a baby involved? I had told Claire about it several years after it had happened, did she tell him?

I said "thank you, it was a devastating loss, but we were able to heal after time went on." Then he told me that he figured out the timing on the pregnancy and that if it was Max's baby then I was quite the liar when it came to my feelings for him at the time.

What a wedding gift I was getting from him after all of these years. The one time that I didn't want to see him, this is what gets talked about.

I felt like I didn't owe him an explanation, because several years have gone by and at the time I wasn't going to trap him into being with me. I look to see if Max seen who I was talking too and he was too busy dancing with his mom out on the dance floor to see that I was preoccupied.

"Grant, I was almost 9 weeks pregnant when the accident happened. I asked Max to come to my appointment with me, because he was the only one that I could trust." "The accident was horrible and the baby was lost." "The baby was yours." "What more do you want me to tell you?" "I was so hurt by you deciding that you didn't want to be with me anymore that I decided not to tell you, because I didn't want to trap you and give you regrets to why you were with me when you didn't want to be." "I was saving you the heartache." "Is that enough?" "Can you just deal with the honest truth and let me have this night to be with my new husband and to not leave me with unanswered questions?" "I have had my share of heartache, heartbreak, at your expense and tonight, I just want to be happy." "Can you give me that?"

Grant's eyes were watery and he looked as though he was going to shed some tears over the truth of the demise of our unborn baby or maybe the fact that now I was stronger and ready to dispose of him once and for all. Whatever the case maybe? He apparently had a heart.

Max made eye contact with Grant from across the dance floor and I didn't think this would end well. Max came walking over at lightning speed and wanted to know what the hell was going on?

Grant told him that he knew about our little secret and things would be very different right now if he had known that I was carrying his child. He would have been the one coming to my appointment and he would have been a great father if I had only told him.

Maybe I was wrong for not telling him, but I didn't have any regrets at this point in my life. I had learned over the years that I had to keep pushing forward and to not keep looking back at the past. With Grant standing in front of me at this moment, I felt sorry for him. I am sure this was a lot to swallow, but what else did he want me to do? I was standing in my wedding dress looking at the man I had dreamed would be standing across from me saying his vows and now I am standing here in real life looking at him in regular clothes with my husband Max standing next to me.

This was weird and nostalgic all at once. I wonder what he was really thinking and feeling at this moment. Grant started to walk away from me and Max and I looked at Max like this was the time I needed to chase after him just one more time, but I would be back to finish out our dance and our wedding night.

"Grant!" "Grant!" "Will you stop this one time and talk to me?" "What should I say to you?" "All of my life I have been the one talking and you get by without saying what you need to get off of your chest." "It's time that you finish the business that you started and live without regrets." "I have dealt with this lingering memory of you and me together and it never happened." "I am fine with that now, it will never be a reality, because you have the inability to say how you feel when it matters the most." "I loved you, I would have done anything for you, and having your baby would have been special, but I was not going to make you fall in love with me over a child, if that is not how you felt." "Max was there for me when I couldn't let you know about the baby." "I needed him." "He loves me like I was hoping you would and you didn't" "Just let it go and find happiness with your wife."

"Savannah, she died in a car accident three years ago." "I was hoping you hadn't walked down the aisle yet with Max." "I guess I am too late." That explains the hurt in his eyes when I confirmed the fact that our child had died. He has dealt with death before.

"I am so sorry Grant." "I had no idea." I gave him a hug, because that is all I could give him. I couldn't go back again and this was going to be a hard time for him. "Look, I should have told you and I am sorry, but there is nothing I can do to change it." "Go find your happiness now and pretend there was no baby." "I know this is hard for you to hear, but if you truly loved me, you would have let me come to see you that March and I would have told you about the baby and who knows things might have been different." "Now you get to deal with the "what if" and I am going back to my husband that loves me."

"Good-bye Grant" I walked away from him that night to never see him again. My wedding night was amazing and Max was relieved that I didn't run off with my fantasy. I told him there was no way I was going to leave him hanging on his wedding night and that what kind of mother would I be to his child without him. Max was surprised, but knew something was up when I had a little bump showing through my wedding dress. It was still early, but we were going to be welcoming our first child together in the winter months. Max was going to be a great father and this was going to be such a great addition to our family.

Max said he was thrilled to be able to marry his "what if" and finish the business that was started that day in the car. He said he always loved me and knew that someday I would come to my senses and we would be together. Isn't it funny how life works out? I already felt that we had gone through the "better or worse" part of marriage and it was only going to get better from this day forward.

I never thought about Grant again and who really knows what happened to him. It doesn't pay to leave things unfinished and he would now have a little heartbreak that he would have to deal with as well. Time would heal his wounds like it has healed mine throughout the years. I feel a little insensitive, but I have had my share of unhappy moments and several that came on, because of Grant.

I think the best part of love it can happen when you least expect it and sometimes that is the best kind of love. Max and I have a lot of fun together and know that every day we are together is a gift from God. We are going to make our home in the city with our three children and just maybe we will live happily ever after.

When I look back on my life, it feels as though I spent so much time thinking of the unanswered questions and wondering if Grant would ever come to his senses. How pitiful was I?

I have to smile now every time I pass a wheat field and know that at one time in my life there were special things that happened surrounded by the golden color of the wheat. What fond memories I have now of snowmobile rides, wheat fields, and docks. The best part is my heart no longer flutters when I think about this, because the memories that make my heart flutter now are far more special. Like when Max picked up his daughter for the first time, or when he carried me across the threshold into our new home, or when Griffin scored his game winning score at his basketball game, and when Scarlet asked Max if it was okay to start dating.

These are by far the best times in my life and there will be many more to come.

A what if can consume you almost disabling you from finding love again. I tried to stay open to new possibilities and that is when Max came into my life. I highly encourage all of my friends to finish what they have started and to never say never. If love is going to happen it will and sometimes it is out of our control. Fate already knows the paths that we are going to take and it just steers us along. We have to be thankful for every encounter that we get and be even more thankful to know that it was already planned for us.

THE END!!!

Thank you for sharing in this story of lost love and moving on. The story is something that is dear to me, because we all have had a love that just didn't last and you wonder why and what if things were different.

The best part is we are all given the ability to move on and deciding to take that step can take a lot of courage and strength.

Love is remarkable and something that we all should have the opportunity to feel. There is nothing more special than feeling loved by someone.

Hope you all enjoyed this weekend read and look forward to having you all read more of my books in the future!!

Melanie Hendricks-Richert

Made in the USA
Middletown, DE
30 November 2022

16565388R00073